The Berenstain Bears

IN THE DARK

Being afraid
of the dark
Doesn't just happen
to you.
It happens,
sometimes,
To little bears, too.

A FIRST TIME BOOK®

The Berenstain Bears
IN THE DARK

Stan & Jan Berenstain

RANDOM HOUSE 🏠 NEW YORK

Copyright © 1982 by Berenstains, Inc. All rights reserved under International and Pan-American Copyright Conventions. Published in the United States by Random House, Inc., New York, and simultaneously in Canada by Random House of Canada Limited, Toronto. *Library of Congress Cataloging in Publication Data:* Berenstain, Stan. The Berenstain bears in the dark. (Berenstain bears first time books) SUMMARY: When Brother Bear brings a spooky book from the library, bedtime and the dark become ominous and threatening to Sister Bear. [1. Night—Fiction. 2. Fear—Fiction. 3. Bears—Fiction] I. Berenstain, Jan. II. Title. III. Series: Berenstain, Stan. Berenstain bears first time books. PZ7.B4483Berj. [E] 82-5395 AACR2 ISBN: 0-394-85443-8 (trade); 0-394-95443-2 (lib. bdg.)   Manufactured in the United States of America

60 59 58 57 56 55 54

"Brother Bear," said Sister impatiently, "are you going to take all day to pick your books?"

Sister and Brother Bear were at the Bear Country Library. Sister had already chosen her books and was waiting at the check-out desk.

"Hold your horses," said Brother. "I'm looking for a good mystery."

Sister Bear usually took out storybooks and books about nature—and sometimes books of poems. Brother liked those, too, but lately he'd become interested in mysteries—especially spooky ones.

"Hey, this one looks good," he said finally. "Okay, let's check out."

"Hmmm," said Sister, looking at the cover. It was called *The Case of the Crying Cave.* "It looks scary to me!"

"Say! This is really good!" said Brother later that evening when the Bear family had settled down for some reading. "Would you like me to read it to you?" he asked Sister.

Sister was looking at a storybook about three kittens who were arguing about which was the prettiest— and it *was* a little boring.

"Or are you scared?" teased Brother.

"Of course not," said Sister. She left her book on the floor and climbed onto the bench to sit beside him.

The mystery began quietly. It told about some bear scouts who were on an overnight camp-out.

THE CASE OF THE CRYING CAVE

When the scouts discovered a dark, secret cave, Brother's mystery began to get a little exciting. And when the cave began to cry and wail, it was anything but quiet!

"'*Who-o-o-o-o!* cried the deep, dark mysterious cave,'" read Brother with a lot of expression. "'*Who-o-o-o-o!*'"

"Stop!" said Sister, putting her fingers in her ears. "That's enough!" And she went back to her storybook.

"Scaredy bear! Scaredy bear!" teased Brother.

"And that's quite enough of *that*," added Papa Bear, looking up from his paper.

At the cubs' bedtime Papa and Mama said good night, turned off the light, and left the cubs in the usual sleepy darkness.

Outside the tree house the bright, busy sounds of day had given way to the soft, soothing sounds of night—the quiet conversation of frogs and toads, the soft cry of the owl, the sigh of the night wind. And if you listened very hard, you could *almost* hear the softest sound of all—the sound of lightning bugs switching their lights on and off, on and off.

But inside the tree house Sister Bear wasn't even beginning to fall asleep. That night the dark didn't seem the least bit quiet and sleepy. In fact, it seemed like the spooky darkness of a scary cave. And the friendly old chest of drawers and funny clothes tree that Papa had made didn't seem so friendly and funny. They seemed more like cave creatures.

So when Brother decided to tease her a little more by making a wailing noise—a really spooky wailing noise— it gave her quite a scare.

"Mama! Papa!" she cried. "Hurry! Come quick!"

And come quickly they did.

Papa rushed into the dark room and tripped over the clothes tree.

Mama rushed in after Papa and tripped over him.

In the commotion Sister fell out of bed and landed on both of them!

Then Brother, who had started it all with his spooky wail, turned on the light. What a mess! Sister, still scared, was holding on to Papa. Papa was holding on to the toe he had stubbed. And Mama was looking for the nightcap she had lost in the confusion. All three of them were pretty annoyed with Brother Bear.

It turned out to be a very long night in the Bears' tree house. Papa and Mama tried to explain that there was nothing to be afraid of in the dark (except maybe running into a clothes tree and stubbing your toe)—but it didn't do any good.

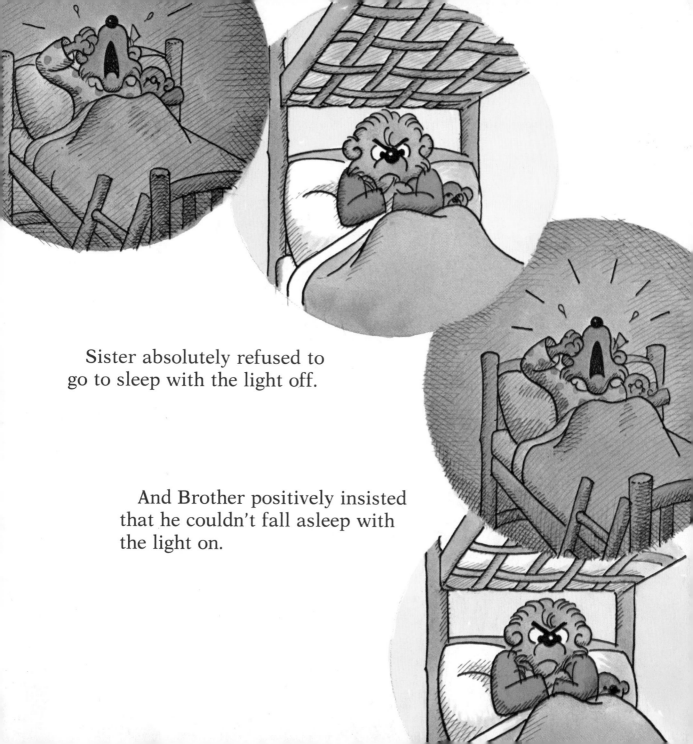

Sister absolutely refused to go to sleep with the light off.

And Brother positively insisted that he couldn't fall asleep with the light on.

The next morning the Bear family was very sleepy-eyed.
"Boy," said Brother, yawning, "I sure don't want to go
through another night like that!"
"Neither do I," said Papa. "And I think I have an idea
that might help."

He took Sister's hand. "Come with me," he said.

"Where are we going?" she wanted to know.

"Up to the attic."

"The attic? But it's dark in the attic—even in the daytime."

"I know," said Papa. "But there's something I want to show you. Anyway, there's nothing so special about the dark. It's just part of nature, like the light. It's your imagination that makes the dark seem spooky sometimes."

"What's imagination?" asked Sister.

"Imagination is what makes us think that chests of drawers and clothes trees are cave creatures."

"I wish I didn't have one," said Sister.

"Don't say that," said Papa. "A lively imagination is one of the best things a cub can have. It's imagination that lets us paint pictures, make up poems, invent inventions! The trick is to take charge of your imagination—and not let it take charge of you."

When they got to the attic, Papa began to rummage through boxes, looking for something.

Sister tried to follow Papa's advice and not let her imagination take charge.

And it worked—a spooky shape turned out to be the shadow of some old tools.

What looked like a giant was really some piled-up furniture.

"Here it is!" said Papa. "My old night light! The one I used when I was a cub and had a little trouble falling asleep in the dark!"

Sister couldn't quite believe that her big, powerful papa was ever afraid of the dark.

"Oh, sure," said Papa. "Most of us are at one time or another."

"How about reading the rest of *The Case of the Crying Cave*?" Sister asked Brother later that day.

"Are you sure you want me to?"

"Sure! I want to see how it turns out!" she insisted.

When it turned out that there was nothing very spooky about the terrible wailing noise (it was caused by wind blowing across an opening in the roof of the cave—like the noise you make when you blow across the top of a bottle), Sister was a little disappointed.

And that night, when she and Brother were all settled down in the cozy glow of Papa's old night light, she said so. "I was pretty disappointed by the way *The Case of the Crying Cave* ended."

"Why?" asked Brother.

"Because," she said, "I was hoping
the wailing would be a really spooky,
scary monster!" And she leaned down
from her bunk over Brother's and
made a spooky, scary monster face
at him.

"*Cut that out!*" cried Brother.

Then Sister went right to sleep.
But Brother lay awake for quite some time
listening to the owl hoots and thinking that
maybe he'd had enough mysteries for a while.